HIGHLIGHTS OF NASCAR RACING™

THE GREATEST NASCAR TRACKS

MATTHEW ROBINSON

rosen publishing's
rosen
central®

New York

Published in 2008 by The Rosen Publishing Group, Inc.
29 East 21st Street, New York, NY 10010

Library of Congress Cataloging-in-Publication Data

Robinson, Matthew, 1978–
The greatest NASCAR tracks / Matthew Robinson.
   p. cm. — (Highlights of NASCAR racing)
Includes bibliographical references and index.
ISBN-13: 978-1-4042-1400-2 (library binding)
1. NASCAR (Association)—Juvenile literature. 2. Stock car racing—United States—Juvenile literature. 3. Racetracks (Automobile racing)—United States—Juvenile literature. I. Title.
GV1029.9.S74R59 2008
796.72—dc22

                                                           2007033802

Manufactured in the United States of America

On the cover: Tony Stewart, driver of the #20 Home Depot Chevrolet, races Dale Earnhardt Jr., driver of the #8 Budweiser Chevrolet, during the NASCAR Nextel Cup Series.

CONTENTS

When the fireworks are going off and the cars are revving their engines, there are few sporting events more exciting than a sold-out race at a NASCAR racetrack.

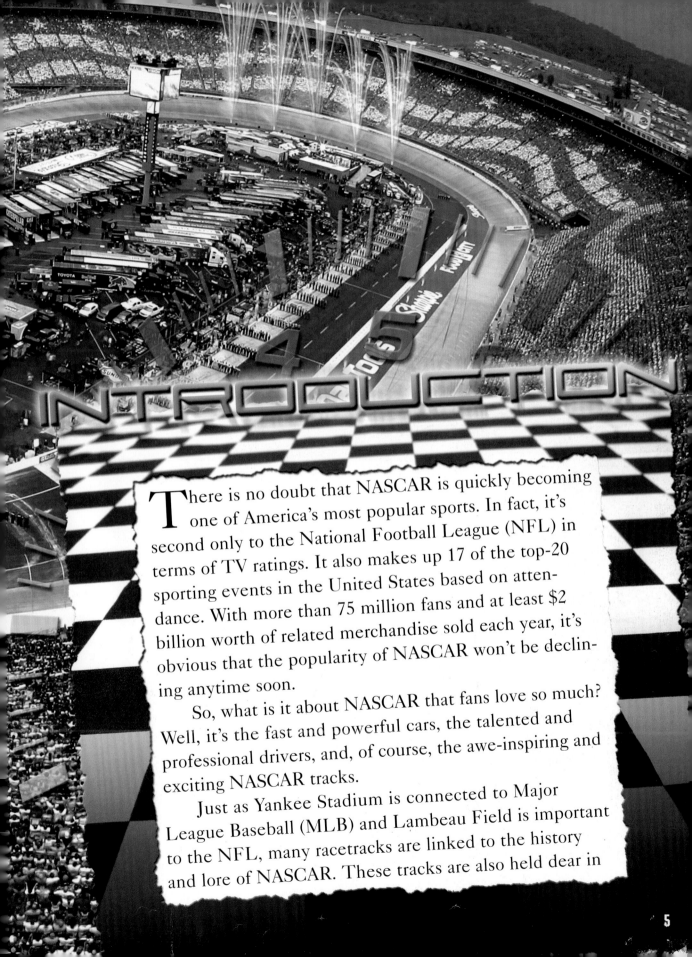

There is no doubt that NASCAR is quickly becoming one of America's most popular sports. In fact, it's second only to the National Football League (NFL) in terms of TV ratings. It also makes up 17 of the top-20 sporting events in the United States based on attendance. With more than 75 million fans and at least $2 billion worth of related merchandise sold each year, it's obvious that the popularity of NASCAR won't be declining anytime soon.

So, what is it about NASCAR that fans love so much? Well, it's the fast and powerful cars, the talented and professional drivers, and, of course, the awe-inspiring and exciting NASCAR tracks.

Just as Yankee Stadium is connected to Major League Baseball (MLB) and Lambeau Field is important to the NFL, many racetracks are linked to the history and lore of NASCAR. These tracks are also held dear in the hearts of NASCAR fans, whether as the tracks where they first witnessed a true NASCAR race or the site of their favorite tailgate parties. NASCAR tracks are where the cars, drivers, and fans come together to share in the joy and adventure of stock-car racing.

Before we get into the specific NASCAR tracks, let's take a moment to understand the different types of tracks as well as a little bit about NASCAR and the sport of stock-car racing.

Stock-car racing is different from other types of racing in that it uses only cars that are in production and sold to the public. Whereas a typical race car would be custom built from the ground up and designed to go as fast as possible, stock cars start out as your basic "stock" cars that you could walk onto a car lot to purchase. These cars are reconfigured to be as fast and light as possible. While the stock cars that are used in today's NASCAR races are considerably different from the cars you could purchase yourself, they still share the same model names and similar bodies.

NASCAR stands for National Association for Stock Car Auto Racing. It was founded in 1947 by William France Sr. and a handful of other race promoters in Daytona Beach, Florida. After its inception, NASCAR quickly became the premier national race promoter for stock-car racing.

There are two main series of stock-car racing in NASCAR: the Nextel Cup Series and the Busch Series. To borrow a baseball analogy, in many ways the Nextel Cup is like the major leagues and the Busch Series is like the minor leagues. If you are racing in the Nextel Cup, it means you are at the top of your game as a driver and are racing in some of the most watched races in the world for huge amount of prize money. If you are racing in the Busch Series, chances are you are working your way up the ranks in the racing world and could soon find yourself racing alongside the big boys.

In this book, you will learn about the many types and styles of NASCAR tracks, which differ in length and shape. NASCAR breaks up its tracks into the following categories:

- Short track: An oval-shaped racetrack measuring less than 1 mile (1.6 kilometers) per lap.
- Intermediate track: An oval racetrack where each lap measures between 1 mile (1.6 km) and 2 miles (3.2 km) in length.
- Superspeedway: Not necessarily a perfect oval (but with only left turns), this track comes in at over 2 miles (3.2 km) per lap.
- Road course: This course has both left and right turns, and it is more similar to a Formula 1–style racetrack that bends and twists with many types of turns.

The tracks you will learn about in this book are five of the most well-known and loved tracks in NASCAR. Some of these tracks are very old, almost as old as the invention of the automobile, while other tracks are much newer, designed with the speed and power of today's modern stock cars in mind. The tracks found in this book host the majority of the biggest and most popular races in a NASCAR season, both in the Nextel Cup Series and the Busch Series.

CHAPTER ONE

Darlington Raceway

Surely, there is no racetrack more steeped in history and legend than the world-famous Darlington Raceway in South Carolina. Sometimes known as "the Lady in Black" or "the Track Too Tough to Tame," Darlington holds the esteemed position of being NASCAR's very first super-speedway.

For many years, Darlington was the home of the Southern 500, a race that was to NASCAR what the Super Bowl is to football. For most NASCAR fans, as well as drivers, Darlington is the true home of NASCAR, the place where they first experienced the high thrills and fast-pumping adrenaline that the sport of NASCAR offers. To most NASCAR fans, Darlington is also the track where they have watched many of their favorite races and cheered for their favorite drivers over the years.

Times have changed since the opening year of Darlington Raceway, but the track's popularity remains the same. While the track may be getting on in years—it is almost 60 years old—it is still just as challenging, feisty, and loved by its fans as it was on the day it was first opened.

The tight and crowded Darlington track can lead to a lot of exciting paint swapping. Get too close to the track wall and you just might earn your "Darlington Stripe," a nickname for the paint you'll exchange.

Track Specs

Darlington Raceway is technically an intermediate track (between 1 and 2 miles [1.6 and 3.2 km] in length) located in Darlington, South Carolina. Although at its inception it was the longest track around (and therefore the first superspeedway), the definition of "superspeedway" has changed over the years, making Darlington an intermediate track in today's terms.

Darlington is 1.366 miles (2.68 km) long and has approximately 65,000 seats. The track is an unusual shape, since it is more egg-shaped than oval, making turns three and four tighter than turns one and two. Since most superspeedway tracks have similarly formed turns on both sides of the oval, Darlington's strange shape makes it a very difficult track for drivers to master.

Darlington is home to two major NASCAR events: the Dodge Avenger 500, which is part of the NASCAR Nextel Cup Series, and the Diamond Hill Plywood 200, which is part of the NASCAR Busch Series.

History of the Track

Darlington Raceway changed racing forever when it first opened in 1950 on Labor Day to a sold-out crowd of 25,000 people. It was the first time anyone had ever seen a high-speed race on a track of that size. For both drivers and fans, it was a day that would forever change stock-car racing. It would lead to NASCAR being the popular sport that it is today.

But how, and why, did Darlington Raceway come to be in the first place? It was all on account of one man named Harold Brasington.

Brasington was a track designer who had a vision of a long, fast track where many could race at once and large amounts of people could come and watch.

Built on top of what used to be a peanut and cotton field, Darlington Raceway was originally designed to be a more traditional oval shape. Legend goes that while Brasington was building the track, a man named Mr. Ramsey refused to move his minnow pond to make room for turns three and four. Therefore, Brasington had no choice but to make turns three and four a different shape than turns one and two in order to leave room for Ramsey's minnow pond. This is why Darlington Raceway has the unique egg shape that fans and drivers alike have come to love. To this day, Ramsey's minnow pond sits just where it did nearly 60 years ago when Brasington designed the track.

Darlington Raceway's immediate popularity was due partly to the fact that there often were as many as 80 drivers on the track at one time in any given race, and partly because the track was long enough to facilitate higher speeds than had ever been seen before. Take 80 race car drivers and give them the ability to drive faster than ever thought possible and you are going to have an exciting spectacle on your hands. Many of the thrills first seen at Darlington Raceway helped shape NASCAR into the sport it has become.

In recent years, Darlington Raceway has been slightly redesigned. Seating capacity has been raised to 65,000, and the front stretch has become the back stretch, and vice versa. While Darlington Raceway was known as being the home of the Southern 500, it has recently lost that title to the California Speedway. Many fans were sad to see NASCAR's biggest race move away from its oldest speedway. However, Darlington Raceway is still home to two very large yearly races: the

Jimmie Johnson leads the field at the start of the 2002 Daytona 500 at Daytona International Speedway.

Dodge Avenger 500 in the NASCAR Nextel Cup Series, and the Diamond Hill Plywood 200 in the NASCAR Busch Series.

What Makes Darlington Unique?

Darlington Raceway is the only track in NASCAR that can say it was America's very first superspeedway. For many racing fans and drivers, it was the home of their first NASCAR memories and the track where they first fell in love with NASCAR.

Darlington's odd, egg-shaped track makes it quite unique as well. Because both ends of the track are shaped differently, it is very difficult for pit crews to prepare the cars to handle perfectly at each end of the track. Even for those who have driven Darlington many times, it still tends to be the track that they find the most challenging.

Famous Races at Darlington

One of Darlington's most famous races was also its very first. On Labor Day 1950, 75 racers were revving their engines and rearing to start the first Southern 500. Out of the field of 75 racers, Johnny Mantz, from Hebron, Indiana, was in the 43rd position—a position most thought nearly impossible to win the race from. By the end of the grueling six-hour-long sporting event, Mantz raced past the checkered flag at 76 mph (122 kph) to secure his first-ever NASCAR win. To this day, no one has ever broken Mantz's record at Darlington Raceway for winning the race after starting that far back in the field.

Darlington's Local Impact

The town of Darlington views

"The Lady in Black"

Over the years, Darlington Raceway has picked up a few fun nicknames. But where exactly do these names come from? The moniker "the Track Too Tough to Tame" is pretty self-explanatory, but where does "the Lady in Black" come from?

At the beginning of every race, the walls that surround the track at Darlington are painted bright white, but by the end of the race, the walls are almost completely black from all the cars hitting and grinding up against them. In fact, first-time racers at Darlington are said to earn their "Darlington Stripe" the first time they slam into one of those white walls.

Known for its level of difficulty and historical importance, there are few tracks more satisfying at which to win than Darlington Raceway, whether you're a rookie or a veteran.

the Darlington Raceway as its main tourist attraction. The second-closest attraction is Myrtle Beach, which is nearly two hours away. The current NASCAR trend of building new tracks in large cities, taking away important races like the Southern 500, has been hard financially for small towns like Darlington.

Because Darlington is considered to be one of the most important tracks in the history of NASCAR, residents of Darlington and racing purists alike hope that NASCAR never forgets "the Track Too Tough to Tame." They hope NASCAR will always keep at least a few of its important yearly races there.

CHAPTER TWO

Bristol Motor Speedway

Racing at the Bristol Motor Speedway, located in Bristol, Tennessee, is said to be like flying fighter jets inside of a gymnasium. Bristol is a short track, meaning that one lap around the track is less than 1 mile (1.6 km) in length. But Bristol is even short for a short track, coming in at only 0.53 miles (0.86 kilometers) per lap. Bristol also has steeply banked turns, meaning that the track is short but the cars don't have to slow down as much on the turns. This makes for fast, short races with plenty of traffic and a lot of cars "swappin' paint," or hitting into each other.

Also known as the "World's Fastest Half Mile," Bristol is world famous for its tense, wild, and unpredictable races. At Bristol Motor Speedway, just the smallest mistake can take you out of the race, but a few good laps could put a trophy in your hand. This is why for many racing fans, Bristol Motor Speedway offers "Racin' the Way It Ought'a Be."

Track Specs

Bristol Motor Speedway can be found in the town of Bristol, located in the northeastern corner of Tennessee. Bristol's oval-shaped track is

The unusually short length of Bristol's track makes for a whole lot of "traffic" on the racetrack, which spells only one thing for race fans: excitement!

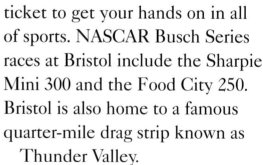

paved entirely in concrete, which allows for higher speeds. The turns are the most steeply banked in all of NASCAR, coming in at 36 degrees on both turns. This makes Bristol much faster than most other short tracks.

Bristol Motor Speedway is home to some of the most popular races of the NASCAR season. In the NASCAR Nextel Cup, there is the Food City 500 and the Sharpie 500, which, due to its extreme popularity, is the hardest ticket to get your hands on in all of sports. NASCAR Busch Series races at Bristol include the Sharpie Mini 300 and the Food City 250. Bristol is also home to a famous quarter-mile drag strip known as Thunder Valley.

Getting Tickets to Bristol Motor Speedway

Bristol Motor Speedway has one of the largest seating capacities in all of sports, coming in at 165,000 seats. Considering how many people the track can hold, you'd think it would be easy to score tickets to one of its popular events. Well, it isn't. In fact, getting tickets to the Sharpie 500, one of NASCAR's most popular races, is nearly impossible. A ticket to the Sharpie 500 is one of the hardest tickets to get in all of sports, second only to the opening ceremony of the Olympics.

History of the Track

Bristol Motor Speedway was designed by Carl Moore, Larry Carrier, and R. G. Pope. It was supposed to be

It's amazing that such a short track can hold so many people—165,000! Even more amazing is how hard it is to get a ticket!

built in the town of Piney Flats, Tennessee, but the locals objected to the project. Instead, Moore, Carrier, and Pope built their tack on top of what used to be a dairy farm in the town of Bristol, Tennessee.

After a trip to Charlotte Motor Speedway, a 1.5-mile (2.4 km) intermediate track, the three men envisioned a short, fast, oval-shaped track that would offer spectators a closer and more intimate racing experience. Taking inspiration from Charlotte Motor Speedway but shortening their track down to half a mile instead of a mile and a half, Moore, Carrier, and Pope set to work on Bristol.

In 1961, when the track first opened, it came in at a perfect half mile. In 1969, the track was redesigned with turns that banked at 36 degrees and increased the track length to the 0.53 miles (.85 km) per lap that it is today. In 1992, the track was repaved, from asphalt to concrete, making for faster and more exciting races.

What Makes Bristol Motor Speedway Unique?

Short tracks are usually thought of as the slowest of all NASCAR tracks. At the same time, they're also considered to be some of the most exciting tracks because so many cars are packed into such a small space. Bristol has the best of both worlds. Because of its steeply banked turns, cars don't have to slow down as much on the turns and, therefore, they can go faster than they would at most other short tracks. Couple this speed with a very short track congested with a lot of cars and you've got a wild, exciting race on your hands.

In the Nextel Cup, there are 36 cars that start each race. The short length of the track puts the cars at the back of the pack almost half a lap behind the leaders before the race even begins. This makes qualifying for pole position (the most favorable position at the start of a race) all the more important at Bristol. Even if you start at the back of the pack, all it takes is a few good moves and fast pit stops, and you can be right back in the action. Meanwhile, a driver who has been in the lead the entire race can have one unexpected pit stop and all of a sudden find himself two to three laps behind, making Bristol a very exciting and unique racing experience for drivers and fans alike.

Famous Races at Bristol Motor Speedway

The first race to ever take place at Bristol was also one of its most famous. The race was called the Volunteer 500, and the car that won

Those 36-degree banking turns and the all-concrete track make for some tight, fast racing. There's a reason they call it "the World's Fastest Half Mile."

it was driven by two different men throughout the course of the race. How did this happen?

The date was July 30, 1961. Jack Smith, from Atlanta, was in the driver's seat of his Pontiac as the race began. Smith competed for more than half of the race, but after 290 laps, he had to have Johnny Allen finish as a relief driver. Both Smith and Allen shared the prize money. It's not often that the winning car of a race is driven by two different people!

Bristol Motor Speedway's Local Impact

Bristol is famous for more than just being the home of one of NASCAR's most popular tracks. It's also considered to be the birthplace

THE GREATEST
NASCAR TRACKS

of country music. This genre of music is a major tourist attraction for Tennessee. People come to the state from all over to attend NASCAR races and enjoy country music.

Around Christmas each year, fans are invited to drive along a route in Bristol that is decorated with holiday lights. The route ends with an actual lap on Bristol Motor Speedway. What a thrill!

CHAPTER THREE

Daytona International Speedway

Daytona International Speedway is home to the most important race in the NASCAR season, the Daytona 500. It is a 2.5-mile (4 km) superspeedway that is located in Daytona Beach, Florida, and it is famous for high speeds, historic races, and huge crowds. Each year, the excitement of NASCAR season is sparked at this track.

Daytona International Speedway boasts one of the largest racing facilities in the world. It features a tri-oval shaped racetrack, a 3.56-mile (5.73 km) road course, and a 29-acre lake known as Lake Lloyd. For many racing fans, Daytona is the true home of everything that is great about NASCAR.

Track Specs

Being a superspeedway, meaning the track is over 2 miles (3.2 km) in length per lap, Daytona International Speedway measures in at 2.5 miles (4 km) per lap. The tri-oval formation gives the track the shape of an upside-down triangle combined with an oval. Both ends of the oval have 31-degree banking turns, while the tri-oval turn

With a track width of 40 feet (12.2 meters) across and 31-degree banking turns, cars can keep their high speeds and still run tight in a pack at Daytona.

banks at 18 degrees. Because of the long and straight sections in the track, stock car speeds can average above 170 miles (274 km) per hour.

The NASCAR Nextel Cup Series races at Daytona include the Daytona 500 (considered by many to be the most important race in the season), the Pepsi 400, the Bud Shootout, and the Gatorade Duel. In the NASCAR Busch Series races at Daytona, you can find the Orbitz 300 and the Winn-Dixie 250.

History of the Track

In 1947, NASCAR was founded by William France Sr. and a few other race promoters in Daytona Beach, Florida. Just ten years later, in the very same city, construction began on what would eventually become NASCAR's most important track, the Daytona International Speedway.

When building the track, the dirt used to elevate the banked turns was taken from the middle of the track. Instead of filling that hole back in with dirt, the builders decided to fill it with water instead and create a man-made lake, which is known today as Lake Lloyd. But the lake isn't just there to look pretty; it's used for high-speed, exciting powerboat racing as well.

The restrictor plates installed in all cars that race at Daytona insure a safe, exciting event for both drivers and fans alike.

On February 22, 1958, Daytona International Speedway was opened to the public. Forty-one thousand people attended the first race. Today, Daytona can hold as many as 167,785 people—and on NASCAR racing days, it always does.

In 1998, lights were installed for Daytona's very first nighttime race: the Pepsi 400. It took so many lights to illuminate the 2.5-mile-long track that Daytona's lighting system became the largest outdoor lighting system in the world.

What Makes Daytona International Speedway Unique?

Safer Racing

Many people compare Daytona to Talladega because they are arguably NASCAR's most popular superspeedways. But there are some big differences between the two tracks. Daytona is a much narrower track than Talladega, forcing cars to spread out a bit and not drive so close to one another. Because of this, there are far less crashes and pileups at Daytona than there are at Talladega. This makes Daytona more about car handling and less about "the Big One"—a racing term for a giant, multiple-vehicle car crash.

What makes Daytona so unique is that it kicks off every NASCAR season with some of the most thrilling and important races of the entire year. If you're watching a NASCAR race at Daytona, it most likely means that the season is just beginning and the good times are just starting to roll.

Daytona kicks off the NASCAR season with a bunch of exciting races such as the

The Daytona 500 is historically the most watched race of the NASCAR season. Past winners include Dale Earnhardt, Richard Petty, A. J. Foyt, and Mario Andretti.

Budweiser Shootout, the Gatorade Duels, and the Chevy Silverado HD 250. However, the most exciting race of the season-opening festivities is the Daytona 500, also known as "the Great American Race." The Daytona 500 is considered the most important race in all of NASCAR.

What also makes Daytona unique is that cars are required to use restrictor plates to keep from going too fast and causing dangerous crashes on the high-banking turns. A restrictor plate is basically a device that is installed in the car to limit the vehicle's top speed. The only other track on the NASCAR circuit to require restrictor plates is Talladega.

Famous Races at Daytona InternationalSpeedway

One of Daytona's most famous races was also probably its most tragic. In 2001, Dale Earnhardt Sr. died in a fatal crash on the last lap of the Daytona 500. Earnhardt won 76 races and 7 championships in the Winston Cup Series (now called the Nextel Cup Series). He was one of the greatest racers to ever grace the sport, and his death was a painful and powerful blow to racing fans everywhere.

To this day, fans can be seen holding three fingers in the air— Earnhardt's racing number was three—on the third lap of every NASCAR Nextel Cup race.

Daytona International Speedway's Local Impact

Because of Daytona International Speedway's reputation as the "World Center of Racing," it has become a major tourist attraction for the city

Dale Earnhardt Sr. remains one of NASCAR's most beloved drivers. He will always be remembered as one of the best drivers to ever grace a NASCAR track.

of Daytona, Florida. The eight major weekends of racing activity bring millions of people to the track annually. In addition, Daytona USA, a museum that opened in 1996 and that is dedicated to the history of Daytona and stock-car racing, brings a massive amount of tourists to the track all year long.

One of the most popular attractions at Daytona USA is the collection of Daytona 500 winning cars. Each year, the car that wins the Daytona 500 is placed in the museum, giving fans a chance to see it up close for themselves.

CHAPTER FOUR

Indianapolis Motor Speedway

Located in Speedway, Indiana, the Indianapolis Motor Speedway is the largest sporting facility ever built by man. It is also home to the world's most famous racing event, the Indianapolis 500, which is commonly referred to as the Indy 500 or "the Greatest Spectacle in All of Racing." The Indy 500 doesn't allow stock cars (the type of race cars used in NASCAR races). But the Indianapolis Motor Speedway made room for NASCAR racing in 1994 when it introduced the Allstate 400 at the Brickyard, one of the most important and popular races of the NASCAR season.

Track Specs

Indianapolis Motor Speedway is a superspeedway coming in at 2.5 miles (4 km) per lap. The track is in the shape of a rectangular oval, meaning it is primarily oval with a slightly rectangular shape at both ends. The turns bank at nine degrees, which help cars maintain higher speeds around the bends. Originally, Indianapolis Motor Speedway was paved completely with bricks; this fact earned it the

For drivers at the Indianapolis Motor Speedway, when they see that three-foot-long strip of bricks coming at them it's time to speed up and prepare for victory.

nickname "the Brickyard." Today, however, the track is almost entirely paved in asphalt, save for a small 3-foot-long (.9-meter) strip of bricks at the start/finish line. Aside from the repaving of the track, the dimensions of the Brickyard have remained nearly unchanged since it was first built.

The entire facility is more than 559 acres in size and has a seating capacity of more than 250,000 people. This means that not only is it the largest racetrack on the planet, but it is also the largest sporting facility ever built by man. The course is so big that it even contains a golf course called the Brickyard Crossing.

Indianapolis Motor Speedway

Indianapolis has held over 220 races since its inception in 1909. It is also the only track to have hosted IndyCar, Formula 1, and NASCAR events all in the same year.

History of the Track

Built in 1909, the Indianapolis Motor Speedway was the first racing facility to ever use the word "speedway" in its name. It is the second-oldest racing track in the world, the first being the Milwaukee Mile in Milwaukee, Wisconsin.

When the track was first opened in August 1909, it was paved with crushed stone and tar. The track's very first race was canceled halfway through because of injuries and deaths caused by these unsafe driving materials that were used to pave the track. Carl G. Fisher, one of the Indianapolis Motor Speedway's original investors, led the way toward paving the entire 2.5-mile (4 km) track with 3.2 million bricks. The Brickyard became a great success, quickly leading to the track's first-ever 500-mile (805 km) race on May 30, 1911.

In 1961, the track was repaved with asphalt. This left just a small strip of brick at the start/finish line to help commemorate its roots as the Brickyard. Between 1919 and 1993, the Indianapolis 500 was the only annual race held at the Indianapolis Motor Speedway. In 1994, NASCAR came to the track with the Allstate 400 at the Brickyard. The race is more commonly known as the Brickyard 400. Today, the track

Between the years 1919 and 1993, the Indy 500 was the only race held at the Indianapolis Motor Speedway. It wasn't until 1994 that NASCAR came to the Brickyard.

is home to the Indianapolis 500, the U.S. Grand Prix, and the Brickyard 400.

Between 1909 and 2006, there were more than 222 races at the Indianapolis Motor Speedway, and most fans hope there will be many more to come.

What Makes Indianapolis Motor Speedway Unique?

Aside from being a NASCAR track not originally built for stock-car racing, the Indianapolis Motor Speedway is unique because it is steeped in so much racing history. Just the name of its most famous race, the Indy 500, conjures up images of racing glory, history, and prestige.

From its three feet of commemorative brick paving the start/finish line, to the garage area on the track known as Gasoline Alley, to its title as the largest sporting facility in the universe, the Indianapolis Motor Speedway is about as unique and awe-inspiring as racing tracks come.

Famous Races at Indianapolis Motor Speedway

With around 80,000 spectators in the stands, the very first 500-mile (800 km) race at the Indianapolis Motor speedway took place on Memorial Day, May 30, 1911. Averaging more than 70 miles (113 km) per hour, Ray Harroun won the race and gave fans, who paid an admission fee of $1 per person, the thrill of a lifetime.

Indianapolis Motor Speedway Local Impact

One of Indianapolis's most popular events is the yearly half-marathon, 2.5 miles (4 km) of which take place on the actual motor speedway. The

First Indianapolis Motor Speedway Racers

Since 1994, when NASCAR racing first came to the Indianapolis Motor Speedway, there have been nine drivers who have raced in both the Indy 500 and NASCAR'S Allstate 400 at the Brickyard. These racers are John Andretti, Geoff Brabham, A. J. Foyt, Larry Foyt, Robby Gordon, Jason Leffler, Scott Pruett, Tony Stewart, and Danny Sullivan. These are the only racers in the world who can say they have raced in two of the world's biggest races at the Indianapolis Motor Speedway in two different racing leagues using two different kinds of cars!

33

13-mile (21 km) mini-marathon is a part of the 500 Festival, an Indianapolis festival celebrating the Indy 500. For fans of the Indianapolis Motor Speedway, getting to run (or walk) an entire lap on the track is a huge draw. After all, Indianapolis isn't just a famous racetrack, it's also a National Historic Landmark. Added to the National Register of Historic Places in 1975, Indianapolis is the only such historic landmark in all of racing.

CHAPTER FIVE

Talladega Superspeedway

Talladega Superspeedway is all about breathtaking speeds, major intensity, and extreme excitement. This 2.66-mile (4.3-km) track is located in Lincoln, Alabama. (Lincoln is a city in the county of Talladega.) It is the longest, oval-shaped track in the NASCAR Nextel Cup Series. The length of the track allows for cars to reach extremely high speeds throughout any given race. In fact, Talladega is so fast that it's not unusual for cars to hit speeds near 200 miles per hour (322 kph) during a race.

Not only is the track long, but it's wide as well. It's wide even in the turns, which can lead to rows of cars all racing at breakneck speeds right next to each other, often three to four rows deep across the track. All of these cars racing in such close proximity and at such high speeds make Talladega all about action-packed, edge-of-your seat racing. This is exactly why Talladega Superspeedway is one of the most popular tracks in all of NASCAR.

Track Specs

Talladega Superspeedway, the longest track in the NASCAR Nextel Cup Series, boasts some impressive stats. It is 2.66 miles (4.3 km) long.

Driver #24 in the DuPont Chevrolet, Jeff Gordon, leads the pack during a perfect day of NASCAR racing at Talladega.

The track was built in a tri-oval formation, meaning the track resembles an oval that comes to a dull point on the bottom stretch. As a result, Talladega has some very steep banking turns for such a long, fast course. With both major turns on the oval banking at roughly 33 degrees and the tri-oval turns banking at 16.5 degrees, drivers don't have to slow down as much in the turns as they would at a shorter and tighter track.

Because such intense speeds can be reached at Talladega, concerns over driver and fan safety were raised from the very early days of the

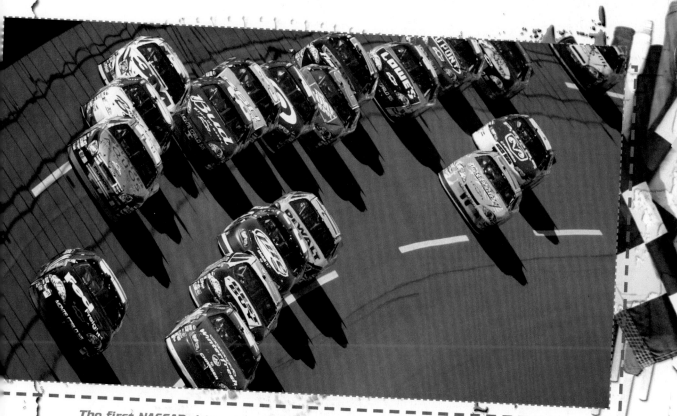

The first NASCAR driver to ever break the 200 mph (322 kph) mark did so at Talladega. On March 24, 1970, Buddy Baker clocked in at 200.447 mph (322.58 kph). Now that's fast!

track's existence. In 1987, NASCAR implemented a restrictor-plate rule for all races at Talladega. The rule was intended to keep the cars from reaching highly dangerous speeds. The only other track in NASCAR to require restrictor plates is the Daytona International Speedway.

The Talladega Superspeedway has a seating capacity of 175,000 people spread out over a 2,000-acre facility. As of 2007, the major races which take place at the track include, in the Nextel Series, the UAW-Ford 500 and Aaron's 499. On the Busch Series side, there is the Aaron's 312.

History of the Track

Construction on the Talladega Superspeedway began in May 1968. The track was built atop old airport runways. It opened to the public on September 13, 1969. The very first race on the track was the 'Bama 400 Grand Touring race. Originally, the track was called the Alabama International Motor Speedway. It wasn't until September 1989, nearly 30 years to the day from its opening, that the track's name was changed to the Talladega Superspeedway. That name is now synonymous with some of the best NASCAR racing on the planet.

Things started out rocky for the Talladega Superspeedway. In 1970, the day before the very first Talladega 500 (one of the most important races of the season at the time), a race car driver's union known as the Professional Drivers Association went on strike because it felt the high speeds and steep banking turns could be potentially dangerous to both the drivers and those in attendance. Even with the strike, the race went on as planned, with replacement drivers taking the place of the scheduled racers.

Another 17 years would pass before restrictor plates would become mandatory at Talladega and speeds were reduced to safer levels. The ruling came right after a racer named Bobby Allison crashed into the Talladega guardrails at 200 mph (322 kph) after blowing out a tire. Allison's car became airborne and nearly broke through the guardrail and entered the stands. Luckily, no one was killed. Because of the mandatory restrictor plates, hopefully no one ever will be.

What Makes Talladega Superspeedway Unique?

Talladega is the only track on the NASCAR roster that allows for so many cars to be packed together so tightly while driving so fast. Many racing fans consider races at Talladega to be the most exciting ones in the world. Not only does Talladega have a high chance of a multicar pileup, or "the Big One," taking place, but any slight mistake can cause a domino effect,

Record-Setting Speed

The fastest speed ever recorded in a stock car took place at Talladega Superspeedway on April 30, 1987. The driver was Bill Elliott, and the speed he reached was a shocking 212.809 mph (342.483 kph). Elliott finished an entire lap at Talladega in only 44.998 seconds. Can you imagine running 2.5 miles (4 km) in less than 45 seconds? Now that's fast!

altering the turn of events for every racer nearby. This makes for some nerve-racking races and some nail-biting finishes.

Much like Daytona International Speedway, Talladega has a mandatory restrictor-plate rule. The rule forces cars to drive at slower speeds in order to avoid dangerous collisions and tire failure. Because of this rule, racing is a bit different at both of these tracks. Cars handle differently when they are fitted with restrictor plates. Not only do they have lower top speeds, but they take longer to reach high speeds as well. To succeed at Talladega, drivers have to adapt to a style of racing known as restrictor-plate racing.

Even with the restrictor plates in place, cars reach higher speeds at Talladega than they do at most NASCAR tracks because the track is so long and the turns are so steeply banked. Imagine how fast they'd go without those restrictor plates!

Famous Races at Talladega Superspeedway

One of the most famous races to take place at Talladega is also one of racing's greatest photo finishes of all time. In 1981, rookie driver Ron Bouchard was in third place behind Darrell Waltrip and Terry Labonte on the final lap of the Talladega 500. No one even saw Bouchard coming as Waltrip and Labonte were neck-and-neck heading to the finish line. Like greased lightning, Bouchard flew by and all three cars seemed to cross the finish line at the exact same moment.

It took a photograph of the cars crossing the finish line to determine that Ron Bouchard, the rookie no one saw coming, was that year's winner of the Talladega 500. Waltrip, who thought Bouchard was a whole lap behind him going into the final lap,

If you're looking for excitement, great drivers, and fast cars, Talladega Superspeedway is the track for you! 'Dega, as Talladega is nicknamed, is NASCAR heaven!

uttered these famous words after the race: "Where the heck did he come from?" It was the only win in Bouchard's career at the Talladega 500.

Talladega Superspeedway's Local Impact

The Talladega Superspeedway is an important tourist attraction not only for the city of Lincoln and the county of Talladega, but also for the state of Alabama as a whole. Visible from Interstate 20, Talladega draws in tourists, racing fans, and tailgaters from all over.

In addition to the track events, the International Motorsports Hall of Fame is located adjacent to the track. Visitors to the International Motorsports Hall of Fame can see some of the greatest racing machines man has ever created.

GLOSSARY

the Big One NASCAR slang for a massive multicar pileup, usually caused from a crash or blown tire.

Busch Series A secondary stock-car racing series in NASCAR that is the equivalent of the minor leagues in baseball.

intermediate track An oval track with a length between 1 and 2 miles (1.6 and 3.2 kilometers) per lap.

NASCAR The National Association for Stock Car Auto Racing. It is the premiere American motorsports association that presides over racing events such as the Nextel Cup Series and the Busch Series.

Nextel Cup Series NASCAR's biggest and most important stock-car racing series. It is the racing equivalent of baseball's major leagues.

pole position The best possible position in which a race car can start a race. This position is at the very front of the pack.

qualifying lap Each car in a stock-car race runs a qualifying lap prior to all major races in order to decide the order at the start line.

restrictor plate A device used in race car engines to limit the speed of the race car; it is generally required for safety reasons. Talladega Superspeedway and Daytona International Speedway both require cars to have restrictor plates.

road course The only NASCAR type of track that isn't a traditional oval shape. Road courses wind, twist, and turn with both left and right turns.

short track An oval racetrack that has less than 1 mile (1.6 km) per lap.

stock car A type of race car that usually starts as a standard "in production" car model and is later modified for racing. Stock cars differ from other race cars that are custom built purely for racing.

superspeedway A racetrack with a length greater than 2 miles (3.2 km) per lap.

swappin' paint NASCAR slang for when two cars touch, bump, or hit each other while racing.

tri-oval A racetrack shape that resembles a cross between an oval and a triangle. Usually the bottom portion (where the pit crews are located) is the triangular section, while the rest of the track is a more traditional oval shape.

Canadian Association for Stock Car Auto Racing (CASCAR)
9763 Glendon Drive
Komoka, ON N0L 1R0
Canada
(519) 641-1214
CASCAR is the organization that officiates Canadian stock-car racing.

Indy Racing League
4565 West 16th Street
Indianapolis, IN 46222
(317) 492-6526
Web site: http://www.indycar.com
Indianapolis, Indiana, is home to the Indy Racing League, which also
        holds events at the Indianapolis Motor Speedway.

NASCAR National Racing Commission
1801 West International Speedway Boulevard
Daytona Beach, FL 32114
(386) 253-0611
Web site: http://www.nascar.com
NASCAR is the organization that officiates American stock-car racing.

Web Sites

Due to the changing nature of Internet links, Rosen Publishing has
developed an online list of Web sites related to the subject of this book.
This site is updated regularly. Please use this link to access the list:

http://www.rosenlinks.com/hnr/grtr

FOR FURTHER READING

Alison, Liz, and Darrell Waltrip. *The Girl's Guide to NASCAR.* Brentwood, TN: Center Street, 2006.

Buckley Jr., James. *Eyewitness: NASCAR.* New York, NY: DK Publishing, 2005.

Canfield, Jack, Mark Victor Hanson, and Matthew E. Adams. *Chicken Soup for the Soul NASCAR Xtreme Race Journal for Kids.* Deerfield Beach, FL: HCI, 2005.

Edelstein, Robert. *NASCAR Generations: The Legacy of Family in NASCAR Racing.* New York, NY: HarperCollins, 2000.

Garner, Joe. *Speed, Guts, and Glory: 100 Unforgettable Moments in NASCAR History.* New York, NY: Warner Books, 2006.

Mara, William P. *Pro Stock Car Racing.* Mankato, MN: Capstone High/Low Books, 1999.

Martin, Mark. *NASCAR for Dummies.* Foster City, CA: IDG Books Worldwide Inc., 2000.

Poole, David. *NASCAR Essential: Everything You Need to Know to Be a Real Fan!* Chicago, IL: Triumph Books, 2007.

BIBLIOGRAPHY

Ahuja, Jay. *Speed Dreams: A Guide to America's 23 NASCAR Tracks.* New York, NY: Citadel, 2002.

Buckley Jr., James. *Eyewitness: NASCAR.* New York, NY: DK Publishing, 2005.

Garner, Joe. *Speed, Guts, and Glory: 100 Unforgettable Moments in NASCAR History.* New York, NY: Warner Books, 2006.

Mara, William P. *Pro Stock Car Racing.* Mankato, MN: Capstone High/Low Books, 1999.

McLaurin, Jim. *Then Junior Said to Jeff . . . : The Best NASCAR Stories Ever Told.* Chicago, IL: Triumph Books, 2006.

INDEX

THE GREATEST NASCAR TRACKS

About the Author

Matthew Robinson lives in Los Angeles, California, and grew up around cars of all shapes and models. He has always been fascinated with the world of motorsports, especially NASCAR. Robinson's favorite racer is Jeff Gordon.

Photo Credits

Cover, pp. 4–5, 9 (inset), 12, 16 (top), 17, 22, 27, 30, 31, 36, 37, 41 © Getty Images;p. 3 © www.istockphoto.com/Jason Lugo; pp. 13, 16 (bottom), 24, 33, 39 © www.istockphoto.com/Simon Podgorsek; pp. 14, 19 © Getty Images for NASCAR; p. 23 © Icon Sports Media; pp. 25, 32, 39 (inset) © AP Photos.

Designer: Nelson Sá; **Editor:** Nicholas Croce
Photo Researcher: Marty Levick